JOHN HAWKINSON
Picture Books

**THE OLD STUMP
ROBINS AND RABBITS
WHERE THE WILD APPLES GROW
WHO LIVES THERE?
WINTER TREE BIRDS**

THE MOUSE THAT FELL OFF THE RAINBOW

Story and pictures by John Hawkinson

Albert Whitman & Company, Chicago

Standard Book Number 8075-5296-8   Library of Congress Card Number 75-150802   © Copyright 1971 by John Hawkinson
Published simultaneously in Canada by George J. McLeod, Limited, Toronto   Lithographed in U.S.A.

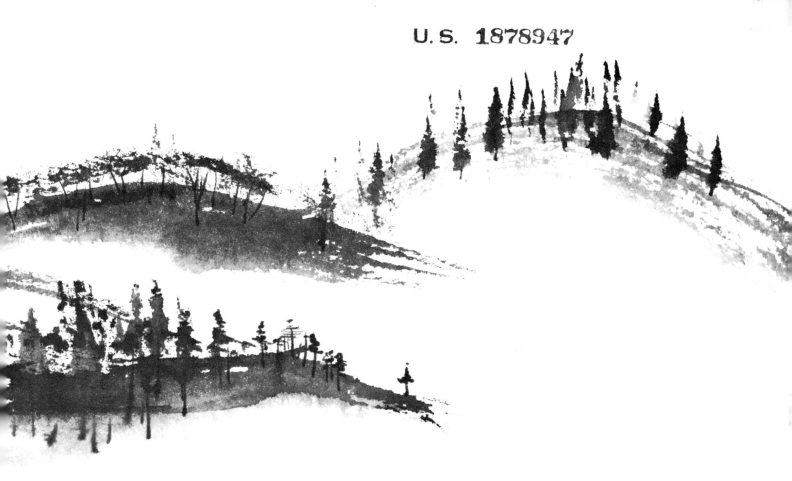

A long time ago, when the world was very young,
no animal, fish, or bird lived here. There were
just trees, streams, and flowers, and miles and miles
of hills and woods.

And there were rivers, lakes, and vast silent
oceans.

One day there was a terrible rainstorm.
It rained for many days and many nights.

And then it stopped, and a beautiful rainbow
came out and reached way across the sky.

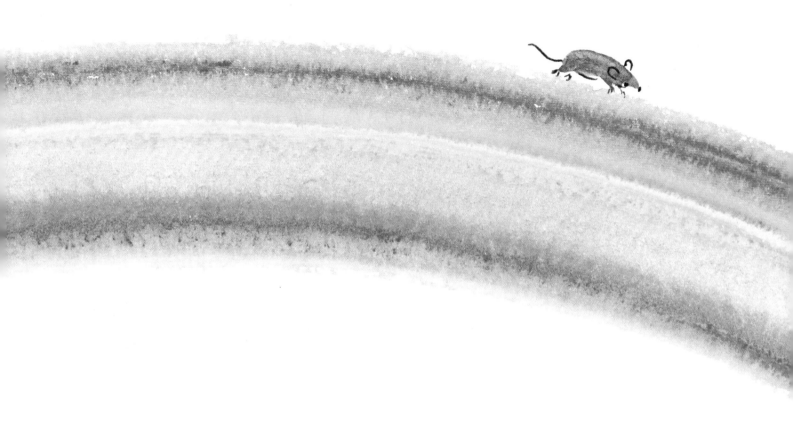

And on the rainbow, a little mouse was running.
Before the mouse could reach the end of the rainbow,
it faded, and the mouse fell down and landed on the earth
in a soft bed of pine needles.

He snuggled down and went to sleep.

The next morning, the little mouse woke up and saw
flowers and trees and soft green moss. He ran around,
climbed up little trees, sniffed flowers, and stuffed
tasty seeds in his mouth.

Then the mouse noticed a big hill.

"I shall climb the hill and see everything," he said.

He climbed and climbed, but it was too far to the top.

A hollow log looked like a nice place to rest. He went inside and fell asleep.

The little mouse dreamed that he had long legs and could jump over a log and reach the top of the hill in no time at all.

As the mouse dreamed inside the log,
a rabbit with long ears and long legs
appeared. He sniffed in the hollow log,
but the little mouse slept soundly.

The mouse didn't see the rabbit hop
away to the top of the hill.

Ahead of him, the rabbit saw more
hills to climb.

Finally the rabbit came to
a forest that was deep and dark.
He was afraid to go in there.
He wished he could see in the
dark, like a skunk or a bat or
a ring-tailed cat.

Up in a tree, a ring-tailed cat
awoke and went into the dark wood.
He jumped from tree to tree, hardly
ever touching the ground.

At the edge of a stream, the forest
stopped.

The cat looked at the water and
said to himself, "If my tail were flat
instead of long and fluffy, it would
help me swim."

Down below, a beaver slapped his tail on the water and swam across the stream.

The other side of the stream had a very steep bank, slippery with clay. The beaver tried many times to climb the bank, but he always slid back into the stream.

He looked up at the bank and thought, "The only way to get up there is in one big hop." And the beaver dived under the water and swam away.

Pretty soon, a big bullfrog jumped out of the stream and up on the bank in one long leap.

The frog took four more big leaps, sat down, and sniffed the air. Something told him there was no water out there ahead . . . only back there.

"It would have to be someone who doesn't like water to go that way," he said as he jumped back into the stream.

Up on the bank, a kangaroo sat munching the grass.
He bounded off. After a long time and many bounds, he
came to a thicket so thick he couldn't get through.

"That's too thick for me," he said. "It would take
a snake to get through that." And he turned around
and munched some grass.

From a little round hole nearby, a shiny black
head appeared. Then the rest of the snake came out
and wiggled through the thicket.

It was only a small thicket. On the other side,
the ground was hard and scratchy. It hurt the
snake's belly, so he coiled up and went to sleep.

And the snake dreamed there was an animal that could go over the hot, scratchy land . . . an animal like an antelope with long legs and sharp hoofs that could run like the wind.

This antelope came to a big cliff. He looked up and said, "It would take wings to get up there." And he turned and bounded away as fast as the wind.

From the grass where the antelope had stood, an eagle rose and soared up and up until he reached the cliff top.

The eagle looked and saw
the ocean. He thought, "I shall
fly way out to the middle and
see everything there is to see."

And the eagle flew all day and all night, and the next morning
he was very tired and there was no place to rest.

"It would take a big animal that could swim for days
and days to cross this ocean," the eagle said.

A whale came up out of the ocean to bask in the sun.
The eagle fluttered down to the whale's back and rested.

The eagle flew back to the cliff, and the whale swam all the way across the ocean and bumped into the other side, where the land began again.

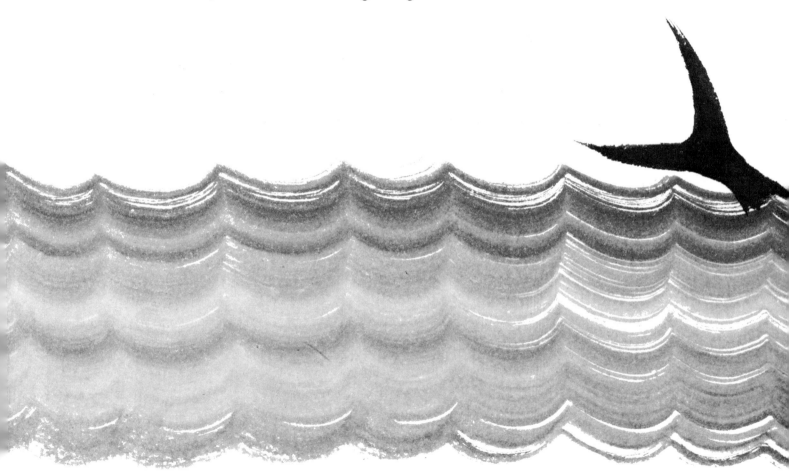

The whale could see with half an eye that the land was very hot and dry. "Anything that goes that way would have to carry water to drink," he figured.

And the whale closed his eyes and let the cool waves roll around him.

Nearby, beneath a mound of sand, two small holes appeared, then two soft brown eyes looked out. A beautiful camel stood up and shook the sand off his hump. He walked slowly over the desert.

The sun rose and burned all day in the sky. The camel walked and walked.

Thorny bushes appeared here and there in the desert. They became thicker and thicker, and the camel stopped. He could go no further.

"Why," he said, "I would have to have a rhinoceros hide (whatever that is) to go through these awful thorns. Look at me—I'm all scratched."

And he sat down and wept.

What looked like a pile of gray rocks rose and lumbered off
into the thorny thicket. For a long time, the animal went through
with ease, stopping now and then to munch happily on the thorns.

But the thicket became thicker, and finally he gave up. He
looked at his scratched hide.

"My goodness! To get through these thorns, I should be much
smaller and have a hard shell over me," he said.

"You mean like me?" asked a little box turtle.

"Yes, and good-bye," said the rhinoceros, turning around.

The little turtle crawled slowly through the thicket for about three feet, which took him about three days.

Then the thorny thicket stopped, and there were grass and flowers and trees.

The turtle crawled through the cool grass, enjoying the smells, until he bumped into a log.

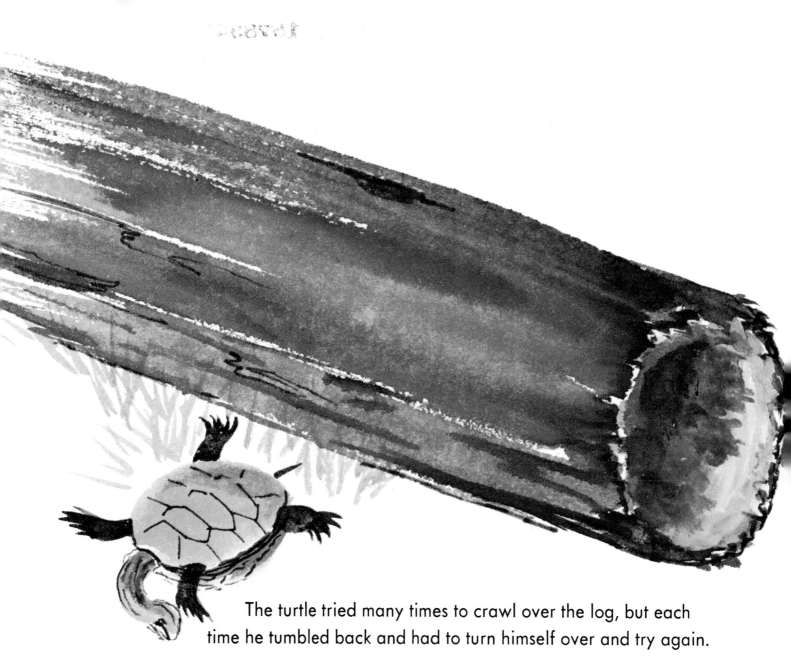

The turtle tried many times to crawl over the log, but each time he tumbled back and had to turn himself over and try again.

The turtle finally gave up. He pulled in his feet, his tail, and his head and went to sleep.

He dreamed he was small and light and had no heavy shell to carry.

From under a mushroom two beady eyes peeked out.

Then quick as a flash, a little brown mouse jumped on the
back of the turtle and over the log.

He landed on the other
side in a bed of strawberries.
He dashed from berry to berry.
His whiskers dripped with red
juice. At last he could eat no
more.

The little mouse found an
opening in the log and crawled
inside for a cool place to rest.

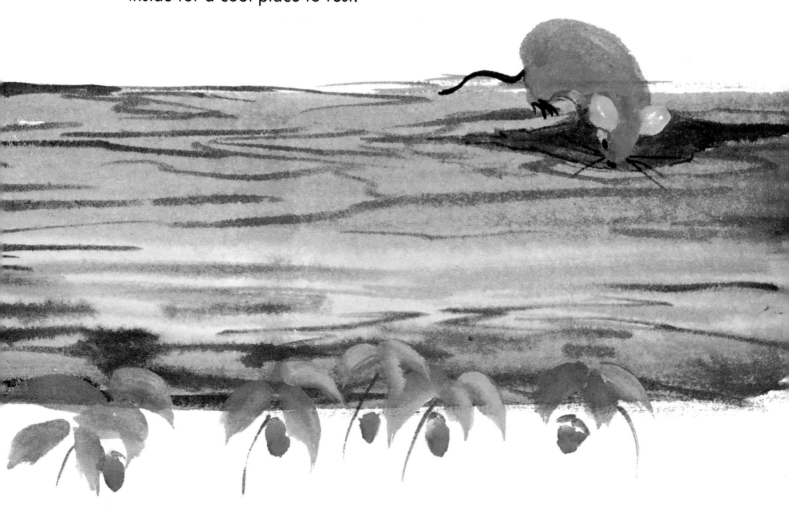

It was dark. He smelled something strange
yet familiar. His nose touched something soft
and warm. He snuggled down and went to sleep.

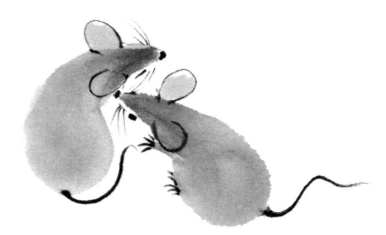